With the timeless characters of RICHARD S

In a Pickle

adapted by Natalie Shaw
based on the screenplay
"The Missing Pickle Car Mystery"
written by Pete Sauder

Simon Spotlight
New York   London   Toronto   Sydney

SIMON SPOTLIGHT
An imprint of Simon & Schuster Children's Publishing Division
1230 Avenue of the Americas, New York, New York 10020
Busytown Mysteries™ and all related and associated trademarks are owned by Cookie Jar Entertainment Inc. and
used under license from Cookie Jar Entertainment Inc. © 2010 Cookie Jar Entertainment Inc. All Rights Reserved.
SIMON SPOTLIGHT and colophon are registered trademarks of Simon & Schuster, Inc.
For information about special discounts for bulk purchases, please contact Simon & Schuster Special Sales
at 1-866-506-1949 or business@simonandschuster.com.
Manufactured in the United States of America 1110 LAK
10 9 8 7 6 5 4 3
ISBN 978-1-4169-9183-0

It was a bright, sunny morning in Busytown. Huckle and Sally Cat and their friend Lowly Worm were headed to the Busytown Park to play.

Once they found a nice spot, Sally took out her jump rope. Huckle kicked his soccer ball around and Lowly Worm relaxed in the shade. Suddenly, the friends heard a yell.

"Oh, dear! Oh, dear!" said the voice. "I can't believe it. It's gone!"

"Let's see if we can help," said Huckle. "Come on, everyone!" They
ran through the park toward the voice. It was coming from the
parking lot.

"My pickle car! I can't find my pickle car!" Mr. Frumble cried. "I parked it in front of these bushes while I went for a walk, and when I came back, it was gone! I just had it painted, too!"

Goldbug, the reporter at the Busytown Action Bug News, zoomed into the parking lot.

"Breaking news!" Goldbug reported from his van. "Mr. Frumble's famous pickle car has vanished!"

"And we're going to help him find it!" announced Huckle.

"Sounds to me like we've got a real mystery on our hands," Huckle said, walking out of the park. He wasn't sure where to start looking for clues, so he asked his friends.

"Who, what, where, when, why, and how," Sally reminded him. "That's how we'll solve this mystery!"

Huckle needed to find out
why the pickle car went missing
and how it happened.

WHO:

WHAT:

WHERE:

WHEN: Today!

WHY and HOW: That's what
we have to find out!

Lowly Worm offered to drive so they could
retrace Mr. Frumble's steps together. Huckle
remembered that Mr. Frumble said that he just had
the pickle car painted.

"Let's start at the paint shop," he suggested.

"Great idea!" Lowly said.

At the paint shop the owner was test-driving a flying car! "What's that you say? The pickle car is missing?" he asked. "Hmmm. All I know is that we painted it *completely* green yesterday."

"Wasn't the pickle car always green?" asked Sally.

"Yes," said the owner. "But now it's completely green. It has green tires, green hubcaps, green seats, and even green headlights!"

On the way back to Lowly's car, Goldbug asked Huckle if he had any more clues.

"Goldbug here for an important update on the missing pickle car mystery. What do you know so far, Huckle?" asked Goldbug.

"Hello, Goldbug!" said Huckle. "Well, we know that the pickle car was painted completely green and that Mr. Frumble left it in front of the green bushes by the Busytown Park."

"Let's go back to the park to look for more clues!" Sally said.

When they reached the park, Huckle, Sally, and Lowly ran into
their friends Pig Will and Pig Won't at the playground.
"Look at the sand castle I built!" Pig Won't bragged.
"You mean the sand castle we built," added his brother, Pig Will.

Sally was really impressed with the sand castle. There was even a bird made of sand!

"How did you make that little bird out of sand?" she asked.

"We didn't!" said Pig Will, confused. "How did it get there?"

All of a sudden the little bird fluffed sand off of its feathers and flew away. It was a *real* bird!

"What happened to the bird?" asked Sally. "I thought it was made of sand."

"The bird only *looked* like it was part of the sand castle because it was the same color," Huckle said, "and because it had sand on its feathers."

"Oh, I see!" said Lowly. "It was camouflaged."

"Camel-what?" asked Pig Will.

"Camouflaged," Lowly explained, "means that something is disguised because it is the same color as everything around it. That's why the bird looked like part of the sand castle."

Seeing the bird fly away reminded Huckle of the time he left his soccer ball outside during a snowstorm. When the snow stopped falling, he couldn't find the ball because it was mostly white against the white snow. When the snow melted, the soccer ball was right where he had left it on the grass!

"Hey, everyone!" Huckle exclaimed. "If the bird looked like it was made out of sand because it was the same color as the sand castle, maybe Mr. Frumble's car looks like a bush because it's the same color as the bushes!"

Huckle ran ahead to the parking lot to see if he could find the pickle car.

Beep! Beep! A few minutes later Huckle drove up to his friends, honking the pickle car's horn.

"We did it!" he yelled. "The pickle car was there all along. We couldn't see it because it was camouflaged."

"Mr. Frumble is going to be so happy!" said Lowly.

Everyone cheered, "You solved the mystery!"

The next day Mr. Frumble had his pickle car repainted in bright colors so he would never mistake it for a bush again! "Hurray for Huckle!" yelled Sally.

"Thanks," Huckle said. "But I couldn't have solved the mystery without the best buds in Busytown!"